The
Second Witch

The Second Witch

by Jack Sendak

Pictures by Uri Shulevitz

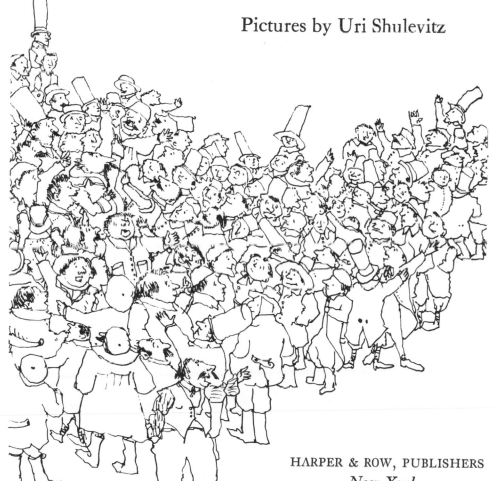

HARPER & ROW, PUBLISHERS
New York

For Gussie

Chapter 1

It started out like any other hot Sunday morning. The cock crowed, the church bells rang, dogs began to bark, and the sun rose lazily in the sky.

Then it happened.

The people of Platzenhausen ran screaming into the streets. Their wailings and lamentations were terrible to hear. And when they looked at one another's faces, their cries grew louder. "A blight has fallen on us," they cried, and they accused one another of being the cause of it. Arguments started which soon led to fighting and even stone flinging. "It is your fault," they shouted at one another. "Your evilness made this happen." But no one really knew the reason for what had befallen them. It was a calamity, a catastrophe. It was beyond anyone's comprehension.

They gathered before the mayor's house. "Help

us, help us," they cried. Surely he would know what to do. Before long the old mayor came tottering down the steps of his house, and the villagers could see that the same affliction had struck him too. He was an old man, Mayor Shrekenhausen, and a very thin man, with skinny little legs that tended to quiver in times of stress. All his strength seemed to be concentrated in his huge moustache that hung magnificently under his thin nose.

The mayor walked among the villagers, who were all talking at once, bewailing their fate, arguing and shouting and sticking their tongues out at one another. He listened, nodded gravely every now and then, and tried to smile as wisely and as bravely as he could. Then he stood before them, with his arms behind his back, and started to speak. His voice was rather scratchy and weak, and the villagers had to listen closely to hear him.

He began by telling them to be as brave and as strong as he was. The villagers took heart. To their grief, however, he added that he hadn't the vaguest idea what had caused the calamity. It was unbelievable. Perhaps, he wondered, he ought to write to the governor or to the king or somebody and find out just what to do. After all, this had never happened before and he couldn't be expected to know everything. Why, he was just as much in the dark as they were. The clamor and the cries of the villagers began once more.

Perhaps it would be wise at this time to tell you just what had really happened on this hot July morning in Platzenhausen.

Platzenhausen, as you may or may not have known, was a tiny village surrounded by a wild and lovely forest. However, the villagers themselves were far from lovely. They were the most unfriendly, unkind, unpleasant people you could ever hope to meet. Certainly you must have heard of the time when one of them fell ill with the measles. Well, he was so upset at the thought that everybody else was out enjoying the fresh air that he invited some of his neighbors to dinner. They came gladly. No one ever turned down a free meal in Platzenhausen. Naturally they all caught the measles. So now they were upset at the thought that others were out enjoying the fresh air, and they invited their neighbors to dinner. Before long *they* caught the measles. They in turn kept inviting neighbors to dinner until the only well persons in the village were those who had had the measles before, and they of course were kept busy taking care of the sick.

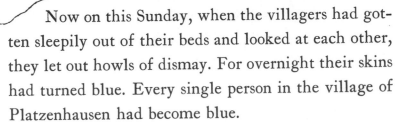

Now on this Sunday, when the villagers had gotten sleepily out of their beds and looked at each other, they let out howls of dismay. For overnight their skins had turned blue. Every single person in the village of Platzenhausen had become blue.

This, of course, sounds very strange and hard to believe, but as you go on reading this story you will find that there was an explanation for the whole thing.

As the mayor went on with his speech Andrew Papenhausen, a little boy, heard the sound of music. It was a very strange kind of music and he decided to investigate. He walked through the deserted streets trying to find where the sound came from. At last he got to the village park, and there under a tree sat another little boy playing on a flute. His skin too was all blue. Andrew watched him for a while. He knew everyone in the village, but he had never seen this boy before.

"What are you doing?" he asked.

And the boy answered, "Playing my flute, of course."

"But why are you doing that now?" said Andrew.

"Because I want to," the other boy replied.

Andrew walked around the boy several times,

listening to the music. Then he said that the music sounded sad. The boy replied that the music was sad because he was sad and that, in fact, he felt very blue. Andrew laughed at this and said that it seemed that everyone was a little blue that day. The boy replied that naturally everyone was blue, because when *he* was blue, everything and everyone around him had to be blue. As he said these words all the trees and houses and streets turned blue too.

Andrew's eyes grew as wide as saucers, and he could hear the cries of the villagers grow louder than before.

"What—what is this? What are you doing?" he screamed.

The little boy didn't answer.

Andrew grasped his shoulder and shook him. The little boy looked up, and Andrew was startled by the strange blueness of his eyes. He quickly pulled his hand away.

"You must stop it. Stop it," he shouted.

The little boy continued to play, and the music became even more mournful than before. Then he smiled faintly and said that maybe if someone could cheer him up, he wouldn't be so sad. Andrew tried quickly to think what he could do, and decided that he would need help. "Stay right where you are," he said, "I will get the others."

He ran back to the mayor's house. The mayor was still speaking, saying that perhaps he wouldn't write to the governor or the king after all, that having blue skins wasn't really so bad, and that perhaps they should leave well enough alone; and he demanded— But here Andrew broke in. He quickly told them what he had seen and heard. The villagers could hardly believe him, but in the distance they too began to hear the sound of the flute. "Follow me," Andrew cried. Away he ran with the mayor and the villagers at his heels.

The little boy was still there, under the blue tree, playing his flute. They all gathered around him and the mayor stepped forward. "Now, now," he said, "what is all this nonsense?"

For a moment the little boy just stared at him. Then he put his flute down and said, "So it's you?"

The mayor, his legs quivering a little, replied, "Me? Of course it is me. I am the mayor and I demand—"

"Yes, I know you are the mayor," said the boy. "I know all about you."

The mayor looked very uneasy, nervously clenching and unclenching his hands behind his back, before he said, "Well, fancy that. However, you must stop all this. I demand—"

The little boy interrupted him again and said that all they had to do was to make him laugh. Then he wouldn't feel blue, and then they wouldn't be blue.

"Well," cried the mayor, "let's make him laugh."

Everyone fell silent. They looked at each other sheepishly. They themselves never laughed much. How were they going to make someone else laugh? What could they do that was funny? Several moments went by.

Then an old lady ran before them. "This should do it," she cried. She proceeded to make what she thought were screamingly funny faces. She stuck her fingers in her ears and rolled her eyes. She pushed up her nose and stuck out her tongue. She was made to stop after a while because, aside from making no one laugh, she was beginning to scare the little children.

Next a man climbed a tree and pretended to be a monkey hanging by his arms and legs. No one even cracked a smile until he slipped and fell on his head. That drew quite a laugh from the villagers, but, alas, not from the little boy.

Some trickster tied a can to a dog's tail. The

frightened animal, trying to escape the racket, ran under a porch where he upset a family of mice. It was a large family and they fled among the crowd. The men held their sides with laughter as they watched the women raise their skirts and scream in panic.

Andrew looked anxiously at the little blue boy. Not even a smile there.

One woman, thinking that now was a good chance to get even with her neighbor whom she didn't like, hit her in the face with a huckleberry pie. Everyone howled except the little boy. The sound of the flute grew more and more doleful.

Some blue pigs escaping from their pens ran squealing among the villagers, and everyone began to fall over each other trying to catch them. It was a scene of mad and merry confusion, but still the little boy did not laugh.

Along came a fisherman trying to balance a fish on his head, but it dropped down his back and he ran off wriggling and giggling. Then a little girl tried to balance a basket of eggs on her head, but she dropped it and she hopped up and down howling and yowling. Another man tried to balance a pail of hot tar on his head, but he dropped it and stumbled away all gooey and gluey. Someone else tried to balance some grass-hoppers on his head and succeeded so well that he couldn't get rid of them at all. He ran around in circles all itchy and twitchy.

Everyone laughed heartily at these antics except the little blue boy, who hardly seemed to notice what was going on.

Someone rang the fire bell. The firemen responded, were informed of the problem, and turned the hoses on the villagers, who frolicked in the water like children. But the little blue boy looked on sadly, and the laughter soon stuck in their throats. What more could they do?

They called the village brass and woodwind orchestra which played as loudly and as gaily as it could. Try as it might, the orchestra could not drown out the melancholy sound of the flute. The villagers danced and sang and tumbled about and shouted with their forced laughter. The little stranger sat in the middle of it all, unmoved and unhappy.

Then someone pulled the mayor's moustache. The little boy looked up. The mayor, caught too in the desperate madness of the moment, threw his arms over his head, broke into a silly dance—on his thin

gone for good. And when nothing more happened for several days, they were sure that he was.

They were wrong. They did not know that this was just the beginning of what was going to be a whole series of strange and terrible occurrences.

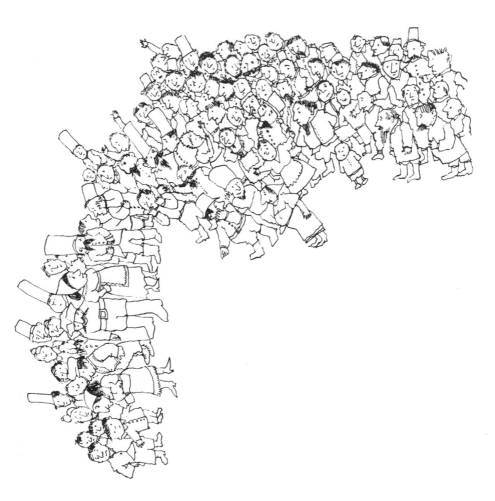

Chapter 2

It was a week later, the day before his mother's birthday, when Andrew went into Ebonhausen Forest to gather some flowers. His mother loved wild flowers, and they would make a fine gift. However, he mustn't tell her where he got them because his parents had warned him many times not to go into the forest on account of the fierce and dangerous bears that lived there. In fact, the only time any of the villagers ever entered the forest was to go hunting and to set bear traps. But Andrew wasn't frightened. He loved this forest. He loved the look of it and the smell of it. And he knew every inch of it too, for unknown to his parents, he went there very often.

Andrew came to an especially dense part of the woods, and as he walked along a very narrow path he could see the witch's house. Of course there was no witch in it now—he hoped. Many, many years ago a real witch had lived there, and she had caused all kinds of trouble in Platzenhausen. Andrew remembered hearing his father tell the story of how the village had finally been able to get rid of her. A child had been killed accidentally through one of her pranks, and as everyone knows, only the soul of an innocent victim has the power to make a witch return to where she came from. It was the soul of this innocent child that finally chased her off. Naturally no one had gone into the house since that time. It seemed to Andrew, however, that he could see some wisps of smoke coming out of the chimney. Probably that was just his imagination. He walked away from the witch's house as fast as he could.

He soon arrived at his favorite spot. Just behind a gently sloping hill was a huge field of wild flowers. It was ablaze with color and the air was filled with a delightful fragrance. How pleased his mother would be with her beautiful gift.

But wait, there was somebody already there. It was a young girl. Was she alone in these dangerous woods? She was a tiny thing with long black hair and a simple red dress. She was very pretty, and although

Andrew was quite sure he had never seen her before, she seemed strangely familiar to him.

Andrew watched her. To his surprise she picked a flower, smelled it, and threw it away; plucked another, smelled it, and threw it away. The boy grew angry. What a waste to destroy these flowers so needlessly. He walked over to the girl and tapped her on the shoulder.

"You shouldn't do that," he said.

The girl glared at him for a moment; then she burst into laughter. Pointing to the flowers, she said, "They aren't any good anyway. See?" She plucked another and sniffed it. To Andrew's utter amazement the flower withered and died.

"It happens all the time," she said, laughing.

"But why?"

The girl would have answered, but there was an interruption. And what an interruption! A huge bear came roaring down at them—the angriest, most ferocious bear that Andrew had ever seen.

He grabbed the girl by the arm and started to run. At first she protested, but he forcefully dragged her along, crying, "I will save you." She smiled and went with him. They raced through the flowers and

15

back into the dense woods. They ran and they ran and they ran—around trees, into heavy brush, even across a small brook. Still the bear came after them, sometimes so close they could feel its hot breath on their necks.

Suddenly—*crash*—the bear fell to the ground roaring in rage and pain. It had been caught in a trap. The boy and girl stopped in relief to catch their breath. Andrew knew that he couldn't have run much longer. Yet seeing the bear struggling vainly in the trap, he began to feel sorry for it.

"I had better go back to the village and get some help," he said. "I don't want that bear to suffer, even though it was lucky for us that it got caught."

"Lucky?" laughed the girl. "That's just to hold it until I can think of something better to do."

"What do you mean?"

"Oh, you wouldn't understand."

"Nevertheless," said Andrew, quite puzzled by this strange girl, "I don't want the bear to suffer. Come on, let's go."

The girl stamped her foot angrily. "I'm not going anywhere," she said. "Anyway, I don't live in that silly village of yours."

"Where do you live?"

"I'll tell you when I feel like it."

"But I want to take you there. I can't leave you here alone."

"I can find my own way, thank you. I certainly do not need your help."

Andrew became annoyed. "You are the most contrary little thing I ever saw. First you ruin all those flowers, and then after I almost saved your life—"

"Saved my life? Is that what you did?" She burst into wild laughter.

"Oh, you are impossible. I am going to get help."

"Go ahead."

Andrew started off, but looking back he was surprised to see the girl smiling as she watched the bear in its struggles. He came back.

"I can't just leave you here."

"Stop bothering your head about me. I live close by."

"Where?"

"I'll show you one day."

"But maybe I won't see you again."

"You will."

The bear growled in pain.

"I must get help," said Andrew. Then he remembered something. "About those flowers . . ."

"Touch my nose," said the girl.

"What?"

"I said, 'Touch my nose.' " She took Andrew's hand and put it on her nose. With a cry Andrew pulled his hand away. Her nose was cold—icy, icy cold.

"Why—" began Andrew.

And the little girl broke into her wild laughter again.

"That's what happens to those flowers," she said. "They freeze up and die when I smell them."

"But . . . why is your nose so cold?"

"Silly. All witches have cold noses."

And with that, she disappeared into the forest.

Chapter 3

As Andrew ran toward the village a sudden cloud obstructed the sun and the air grew chill. After a moment the sun came out hot and bright again. The leaves on the trees seemed to turn greener and the forest became full of shadows. Andrew ran quickly over the scented ground, but as he approached the lake he began to feel uneasy.

The lake was called Lake Merehausen. It was a pretty, blue fresh lake that was the pride and joy of the villagers. Each day, especially on warm July days, everyone swarmed around it swimming or fishing or boating or just dunking in it.

Today as Andrew drew near it he was struck by the stillness, by the strange silence of the place. He could hear the twittering of many birds, the rustling of the great trees, but no voices. No sound of arguments, no splashing, no shouts. On such a warm day, everyone should be at the lake.

Andrew slowed down to a walk. As he turned into the path that led to the water, he felt his heart beating violently. In the quiet it sounded like a drum. There was something electric in the air, some enchantment; as if something terrible was about to happen. Then he saw the lake.

His heart nearly stopped. The lake, pretty Lake Merehausen, was frozen solid. A glittering sheet of ice.

That wasn't all. Most of the villagers were there, as would be expected on this hot day. They were there, all right, but they were statues of ice. An icy tableau, frozen into immobility: There was the mayor, frozen in the act of dunking his feet; Andrew's own friends, frozen as they were fighting or swimming. Imagine! Fishermen, frozen in the midst of fishing; boaters, frozen in their boats. He couldn't look anymore. It was too terrible.

He turned toward the village. There must be some people there. He would call them. He tried to shout, but he couldn't find his voice.

All at once the sounds of wrangling and shouting filled his ears. He looked back at the lake and it was

as though nothing had happened. Lake Merehausen
was blue and rippling; the villagers were swimming
and sailing and fishing and fighting. Everything was
fine again on this hot, sun-drenched day. His friends
called to him and he waved back at them. Had it all
been a dream? Had he imagined the whole terrible
nightmare?

He ran home.

Chapter 4

Andrew couldn't sleep very well that night. He kept reliving all the strange things that had happened to him that day: the icy figures at the lake, the hot breath of the bear on his neck. The bear! He had forgotten about it. Was it still in that cruel trap? Oh, he had forgotten all about the bear. He would have to get help for it in the morning.

And what about the wild flowers? He hadn't picked any for his mother's birthday. And that little girl who said she was a witch, that contrary little girl with her icy nose?

How long the night was. He kicked off his blanket and lay on his back. But his thoughts would not let him sleep. That little blue boy—where had he gone? What was he, a magician?

He lay on his right side . . . on his left side . . .

on his stomach. Nothing helped. He just couldn't sleep.

The church clock chiming eight times jerked him awake. He must have dozed off after all. He dressed hurriedly and had breakfast with his parents. The house was lit up. It was pitch dark outside. "Must be very cloudy today," his father said.

It was nine thirty when Andrew went out, and it was still dark. He could see the villagers scurrying through the streets carrying lanterns. As was their custom, they never greeted one another in the morning. They just slunk past, averting their eyes.

Actually they spoke only when necessary, as when they conducted business and tried to outcheat one another. Or when they got into arguments over the most trifling of matters and would shout and shout. Or when they would rail at the weather when it didn't please them. Or when they bellowed at their children who were having too much fun. Or berated the tax collector when he came for his money.

But today they muttered nervously to themselves about the storm that was coming.

Andrew searched the sky. There was not one cloud to be seen. How could there be a storm if there were no clouds?

Before long the mayor came dashing down the street.

"The clocks—what has happened to the clocks?" he cried. "I demand—"

"It's not the clocks," answered one of the villagers. "It's the sun. It hasn't risen yet. Something has gone wrong with it."

"What do you mean?" sputtered the mayor. "How can anything go wrong with the sun? It must be the clocks. I'll call all the watchmakers and demand—"

"It is not the clocks, Mayor Shrekenhausen. It is the sun."

"Yes, yes," said another. "For the past few days there have been strange things going on in our village."

"Strange things?"

"Yes. It is as though we were in the grip of something. Something evil."

The mayor tugged at his moustache. "Nonsense. Nonsense," he said. "Everything can be explained, I'm sure. All natural phenomena, I'm sure. As for the sun today, why it must be an eclipse. Of course. I'll call for the astronomers and demand—"

"An eclipse! Of course," cried the villagers. What a relief! That explained everything. The mayor

was right: Everything can be explained. They were so lucky to have such a wise mayor.

Just then someone piped up saying he had never heard of an eclipse lasting so long. The mayor replied there was always a first time for everything.

An old lady said that she had seen smoke rising out of the chimney of the witch's house.

"Now, now," roared the mayor. "We'll have no wild tales, old woman. Why, Mrs. Hagenhausen, your eyes are so weak that you can hardly see a hand before your face, let alone see smoke coming out of a chimney. I demand—"

"My eyes may be a little weak," replied the old woman testily. "But my nose ain't. I could smell it."

"The witch has been gone for all these years. I want to know the truth. I demand—"

"I think I saw the smoke too," said a hunter.

The mayor's legs began to quiver. He was terribly upset.

"And I saw," said another, "a little girl running through the woods with long black hair streaming behind her and a great, terrible bear at her side."

Andrew's neck began to tingle.

"Nonsense. Nonsense," cried the mayor. "All natural phenomena, all easily explained. I'll gather all the scientists and demand—" He ran into his house.

At this the people of Platzenhausen went to their homes too. They didn't blame their mayor for being so confused and upset. Who wouldn't be, at such goings-on? They huddled inside their homes and tried to forget their fears by quarreling with each other or spanking their children.

The next morning the sun rose as usual, and the people of Platzenhausen were all very thankful.

Chapter 5

Andrew's legs seemed to have acquired a mind of their own. When he woke up in the morning they would no longer do his bidding. Try as he might to stop them, they led him through the village into Ebonhausen Forest and straight to that terrible house in the woods. The door opened before him and his treacherous legs walked him right in.

The little girl was there sitting on the floor, eating a bowl of soup.

"Come on in, Andy," she said. "Nice of you to come and visit me."

Nice of him to come? What choice had he had?

"How did you know my name?" he asked.

"Oh, I guess you must have told me."

He had not.

"My name is Vivian. You know, you forgot to

pick those flowers for your mother. So I picked them for you. Here," she said, getting up and handing them to him. "They're all right. I didn't smell them."

Andrew took them. They were glorious. But how did she know about his mother's birthday?

"How did you know about my mother's birthday?"

"I think you mentioned it the other day."

He had not.

"Would you like some banana soup? I made it myself."

Andrew shuddered and said, "No." He watched as the little girl sat down on the floor and began eating again. Then, clearing his throat, he dared to ask, "Are you—are you a witch?" The girl looked at him and laughed, a rather frightening little laugh. "Yes, I am, Andy."

Andrew shook his head in disbelief.

"I am, Andy. You might as well get used to the idea. Would you like to touch my nose again?"

"No. No. No."

"You know, Andy, that trick of turning everything into ice? That was just for you. I thought you might like it."

"Like it?" cried Andrew, growing enraged.

"Like it? Why, it was horrible. How could you do such a thing?"

Vivian laughed. "Your frosty-faced friends are so coldhearted to each other that a little freezing shouldn't bother them a bit."

"Then you turned off the sun—"

"Those mean people don't deserve to have a bright, warm sun. Anyway, that was one of my more difficult tricks."

"Tricks? Is that what you call them? You are heartless and hateful. Why have you come to our village?"

And the witch replied, "The people of your village are heartless and hateful. I feel right at home here."

"Well, if you feel so much at home among them, why do you punish them? Why do you do all those nasty things?"

"Because I enjoy doing them. I am a witch. Why, I have a whole list of tricks I am going to play on your village. Every day something new. But you needn't fear; I'll try not to hurt anyone or kill anyone. It's all in fun." She laughed harshly. "Just some practical jokes. Where's your sense of humor?"

"Sense of humor?" cried Andrew, outraged.

"Half the people of Platzenhausen scared to death, and you call your tricks practical jokes. Don't you realize how cruel you are?"

"No, no," came a booming voice behind him. "Vivian is a sweet, wonderful girl."

Andrew was so shocked by the unexpected, powerful voice that he could not bring himself to turn and face it. He could hear the heavy steps of something huge behind him, loud breathing, and the creaking of the floor. Then something grabbed his shoulders and whirled him around. He was speechless with fright.

"You remember me, don't you?" continued the booming voice. "After you led me so cleverly into that trap, Vivian released me and gave me a wonderful gift. She gave me the power of speech and thought. It was the most wonderful gift in the whole world. How can you call her cruel?"

Andrew could hardly believe what he saw. "Gift?" he stammered, looking in astonishment at the huge bear. "You can speak. It's fantastic!"

"I told you I would get even with him," snickered Vivian.

Andrew looked sharply at the witch. Was she joking? She had given the bear a new life. She had

33

performed a miracle. Is that what she called getting even? He tried to smile at the joke.

Vivian looked wryly at the bear, who continued in his booming voice: "Vivian has given me life. I was nothing. I could only rage through the woods, an animal. Now I can think and I can talk and, Andy, I can read. Before long—who can tell?—perhaps the people of the village will accept me as one of their own."

Andrew could hardly believe his ears. The people of Platzenhausen accept him? A bear?

"We've had enough talk this morning," said Vivian, laughing. "Come, Andy, don't be so cross. We are going to be great friends. You'll see."

Friends? With a witch? Impossible.

"And now, Andy," continued the little girl, "let's you and me go for a walk in the village. I hear they are going to have a fair there today and I love fairs. All right, Andy? You and me?"

What? Walk with her in the village? "But," he said, "they might recognize you as the witch and—"

"And you wouldn't want to be seen in my company, eh? You needn't worry, Andy. I'll disguise myself. Oh, I know. I'll become a little cat."

She had no sooner said these words than she did
indeed become a little gray kitten purring at his feet.
The great bear roared with delight. Andrew, who had
seen so many fantastic things these past few days, could
do nothing but shake his head. Nothing could surprise
him now. He knew he could expect anything.

"Come along. Come along," cried Vivian.

Andrew followed her out, glad anyway that his
legs were obeying him now. Hesitantly he waved good-
bye to the bear whose name, he was later to learn, was
Stanwix.

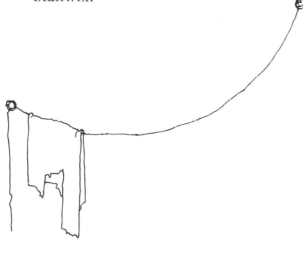

Chapter 6

"Did I hear you speak to that cat?" asked Mr. Grossenhausen.

"I only said, 'Here, kitty, kitty,'" replied Andrew.

"I hate cats, especially black ones."

Andrew looked down at Vivian. She had indeed turned black.

"Why don't you chase her away?" suggested Mr. Grossenhausen.

"Oh, I like cats," said Andrew. "Especially black ones. She followed me all the way from the woods."

"From the woods?" cried Mr. Grossenhausen. "I wouldn't trust anything that came out of the woods nowadays—not with that witch running around wild there. Why, this dreadful cat might be the witch in disguise. If I were you, I would throw rocks at it."

Vivian hissed. And Mr. Grossenhausen's ears began to grow extraordinarily large. He sprouted a tail and began to bray like a jackass. In horror he went galloping down the street and, as you can well imagine, drew quite a crowd.

Andrew looked severely at Vivian, who had turned an angelic white. Putting his mother's wild flowers in his back pocket, he picked up the little kitten and held her in his arms. "Why can't you behave?"

"Are you deaf? You heard what that maniac said. He wanted you to stone me."

"Yes, but you didn't have to change him into a jackass."

"He was a jackass before I changed him into one."

"Oh, Vivian, why must you do such terrible things?" Andrew said, but he could not help smiling.

"I'm a witch," replied the kitten, nestling herself more comfortably in Andrew's arms.

Andrew walked on, holding Vivian tightly and scratching her neck. She was so white, so soft, so gentle. It was still difficult for him to believe that she really was a witch, despite everything he had seen.

They came at last to the fairgrounds. Each year at this time, July the twentieth, a fair was held and all the proceeds went to the orphans' home of Platzen-hausen. Everyone had lots of fun at the fair with the rides, the games, and the shows.

"Let's go in," hissed Vivian.

Andrew obeyed, although he should have known better.

They strolled around the grounds. They came to a magician who was performing before a group of bored customers. He was the town magician, Mr. Hokumhausen, who did this same act every year. Right now he was trying to take a rabbit out of his hat, but something had gone wrong and he couldn't seem to find the poor thing. The audience began to laugh and jeer and throw things. Mr. Hokumhausen became more and more flustered. Suddenly Vivian tore herself free from Andrew's arms and leaped onto the stage. The audience roared with laughter as they watched the kitten run circles around the magician. On the verge of tears from vexation he flung his so-called magic wand at Vivian. She promptly turned orange. There was a gasp of surprise from the audience. The magician was transfixed. Then the little witch calmly changed from orange to green to red to yellow.

Angrily Andrew turned away and left. He should have known; he just should have known. You can't trust a witch. They were going to be great friends, were they?

He walked quickly and was on the point of leaving the fairgrounds when he saw a little white kitten at his heels. For some reason his heart bounded with joy.

"Vivian?"

"Of course, Andy. Why did you run away?"

"You know why. You're always causing trouble."

"Trouble? Why, Andy, I did that for you."

"For me?"

"Yes, because I like you even though you're always so grouchy."

"I am not grouchy. What did you do?"

"Why, those people thought it was the magician that was making me change color. What an ovation they gave him. He was a great success."

Andrew didn't say anything, but he felt better inside. Perhaps someday he might even make Vivian become a good witch. They went back to the entertainment booths.

Vivian insisted that he try some of the games of chance. And although Andrew had never had much luck at them, he couldn't resist anything the witch asked him to do. Maybe they would be great friends after all. Think of having a witch for a friend. The thought filled him with delicious excitement. If the people of Platzenhausen ever found out . . . if his parents ever found out . . .

They stopped in front of a huge wheel. Andrew had to guess what number it would stop at. "Try seven," whispered the kitten. Seven it was. Andrew won a set of dominoes.

At another stall Andrew had to knock down three wooden bottles with a ball. He threw it and down they tumbled. He won a stuffed giraffe.

Then he threw darts at a target. And even though he didn't really try very hard, he hit the bull's-eye every time. Here he won a toy rifle and a pencil box.

He wished he could go on all day like this. Of course he knew that Vivian had something to do with his luck, but he didn't care. He was having so much fun. He hadn't laughed so much in years. It was so wonderful to be there with Vivian. If only he could be with her every day. What fun that would be.

Suddenly a group of boys, laughing, ran by, and one of them grabbed Vivian by the neck and held her down. "Look at this pretty cat," he cried. "Bet she'd look even prettier with a red can tied to her tail." All the boys readily agreed, and many of the villagers

there hooted with laughter. They loved to see such sport.

Andrew stood dumb. He did not know which way to turn. Should he help his friends? Should he warn them of their danger? Or should he help Vivian, also his friend, who was trying to squirm out of the boy's grasp? But before he could do anything, the little kitten began to grow. The boys fell back in dismay. Andrew watched in horrified surprise as Vivian grew bigger and bigger and bigger.

Soon the cat was enormous. The villagers ran screaming in panic as she towered over the houses. And still she kept growing, almost touching the clouds now. She was unbelievably huge.

The monstrous cat turned carefully, as if trying not to step on anyone, although her terrible tail did smash some chimneys, and she headed for the forest. As she disappeared into the gloomy woods she looked back and growled so viciously that many of the villagers fainted dead away.

Chapter 7

It was very early morning. The sun, hazy and wan, rose slowly over the mist-shrouded forest. The fog clung to the trees and the ground like a soft blanket.

Stanwix walked slowly, only slightly disturbing the deep silence of the woods. He carried a book of poetry under his arm. He was so deep in thought that he hardly noticed where he walked until at last he found himself at a familiar spot.

It was here that he had fallen into the trap. It was at this very spot that he had been reborn. Stanwix's great body quivered at the thought of it. Just think! Of all the bears in the world—of all time, in fact—he, Stanwix, had been the chosen one. He was the first animal to become human.

It was here that Vivian, not a witch but an angel, had taken pity on him. Vivian, with her sweet, gentle heart, had freed him with her magic and turned him into a man. Anyway, almost a man. He could think like one, speak like one, act like one. What more did he need?

No longer did he have to stalk through the woods. Now he could live in a house like a man. He could eat at a table. He could sleep in a bed. He could read books. He could discuss things.

And he could understand love, as the poets described it. Did he not love Vivian? Did he not love the forest? And the misty sun? Did he not love his fellow man as the books told him to? Oh, the wonder, the wonderful wonder of being a man.

As Stanwix wandered dreamily through the forest, he came upon a bear scratching his back against a tree. They watched each other silently for a while. Then Stanwix recognized him as an old friend. He approached him, but the other growled menacingly. Stanwix laughed. "Here now," he said. "Don't you growl at me."

The other bear backed away.

"Don't you remember me, old friend? Don't you remember how we used to play together?"

The bear turned and fled.

Stanwix shook his head in bewilderment. "Now,

why did he run? I may be almost a man, but I still look like a bear. I'm still something of a bear."

Or was he? Must he cast his lot only with men now? Must he turn his back on the past? The thought filled him with great sadness. Could he leave this forest? Could he leave Vivian? Must he burn all his bridges?

Well, so be it. The books said that a man must strive for bigger and better things. So it must be with him. He would leave this forest. He would go to the village and live among his fellow men. He trembled. The thought made him feel a little frightened.

The forest came alive with sweet smells and sounds and movements. And the great bear knew how much he would miss it.

He sniffed the air. There was another smell now. Vivian was cooking breakfast. Without another thought he hurried home.

to a child's . . . excuse me . . . to a boy's eyes we grown-ups do and say rather silly things."

Andrew nodded his head in agreement, and then he blushed again. "Oh, sir, I didn't mean——"

"Oh, I know. It seemed the same to me when I was a boy. And, you know, boys change a lot when they grow up to be men."

Andrew went back to his painting, but he was listening carefully. He wondered why the mayor was speaking to him so seriously. Had he seen him and Vivian together? Was it possible? But if that were so, wouldn't he have told his parents? Wouldn't Andrew have been punished by now?

"Yes," continued the mayor. "I know what it is like to have a secret. I remember how life in the village seemed so empty, so unexciting, like an endless dreary dream. Only when I thought of my secret did life become beautiful and real."

"Yes, yes. That's very true," said Andrew, thinking of his own secret. He had always thought of the mayor as a rather silly old man. But now he found himself beginning to like him. "What was your secret, sir?" he asked rather boldly.

The old man was silent for a long time. Then

he said, "It happened so long ago, I'd almost forgotten it."

"Oh, I'll never forget mine," Andrew blurted out.

"I hope you won't. I sincerely hope you won't."

And with that the mayor walked down the street on his thin, shaky legs.

Andrew started whistling again as he applied the white paint to the fence. He was feeling very happy. Everything was just fine. His mother had loved her birthday present. "How very thoughtful and sweet of you," she had said. His father had slapped him on the back and said, "Nice going, old man." Now he had just become friends with the mayor. In the forest there was a fantastic talking bear that he was very anxious to see again. And . . . and . . . there was Vivian.

Suddenly, there was an awful roaring sound. A screaming, violent wind swept down on the village, scattering chairs and papers and tin cans all over the place. The villagers ran for shelter.

Andrew burst into laughter. There amid the flying debris he stood laughing, holding his sides and laughing. It was just too funny. His friend—his secret friend, Vivian—was at it again.

50

Chapter 9

"We must decide what to do."

"We must think of a plan."

"Of course, that is what we are here for."

"Yes, but how can we fight against a witch?"

"I can write to the governor and demand—"

"We can't wait that long, Mayor."

"We must get rid of her before she murders us in our beds."

"But how?"

"We can't chase her away."

"Why not?"

"She is a witch; we can't fight her."

"But we can demand—"

"Maybe if we just asked her nicely to go."

"That's silly."

"What if we gave her some money?"

"Money?"

"Why not? All witches are greedy."

"Money is just the thing."

"But where can we get some?"

"The treasury is empty. Now, listen, I demand—"

"We can all donate some of our own money."

"A good idea, but as it happens, I'm very short of money right now."

"So am I. That wicked witch has upset everything so, I haven't had much work lately."

"Me too."

"I'm broke."

"I couldn't spare a dime."

"But we must raise the money somehow."

"We can use the money we raised for the orphans."

"Oh, that wouldn't be right."

"Why not? What's more important now? Worrying about some wretched orphans or getting rid of the witch?"

"That's so. Let's get rid of the witch before she murders us all in our beds."

"Yes, yes. We all agree. Give her all the money."

"All of it?"

"Yes, all. All."

"We can raise more money for the orphans next year."

"Yes, but last year we used the orphans' money to plant trees."

"And the year before we—"

"That's beside the point. This year we have a witch."

"All in favor of using the orphans' money to bribe the witch say Aye."

"Aye."

"Good. We all agree."

"Now, the next piece of business: How do we give it to her?"

"Mail it?"

"Ridiculous."

"Somebody—somebody will have to take it to her."

"Yes, we must be sure that she receives it."

"We must send someone we can all trust."

"A man above reproach."

"And brave."

"Ah, very brave."

"And able to plead with her."

"And convince her that she must leave."

"There is only one man who can do these things."

"Of course."

"The mayor."

"Now wait, I demand—"

"Yes, and he can deliver the money tomorrow night."

"I demand—"

"At midnight."

"Yes, that's always the best time."

"But wait. She is a terrible witch. What would she want with money? My idea is to demand—"

"All in favor of the mayor delivering the orphans' money to the witch tomorrow at midnight say Aye."

"Aye."

"We could demand—"

"Good! We all agree. The motion is carried."

And so the meeting, in which all of the villagers of Platzenhausen took part, came to an end.

Chapter 10

That night Andrew was awakened by someone scratching on his window. He sat up in his bed and tried to adjust his eyes to the darkness. Soon he could see the shadow of something huge and frightening. What was it?

"May I come in?" whispered the shadow, opening the window and climbing into the room.

Andrew, still groggy from sleep, wasn't sure whether he was dreaming or not. But when he finally recognized the figure of Stanwix coming toward him, he knew that he was awake.

"What are you doing here?" he demanded.

Stanwix looked around the room, at the desk, at the pictures on the wall, at the books on the shelves, at the darkened lamps, at the now thoroughly disarrayed bed.

"Don't move around so," whispered the boy. "You will wake up my parents."

The bear sat down on the bed.

"What are you doing here, Stanwix? If anyone sees you— If my father comes into the room and sees a bear—"

"But that's just it. I want to be seen sooner or later."

"But why?"

"Don't you see, Andy? One of these days I want to walk right into the village in broad daylight and be welcomed—*welcomed*, mind you—by the people as one of their own. And maybe I could come and live here in this very room with you, Andy."

"Live here? Oh, I don't know. I don't know if the room is large enough. And my mother might not—"

The bear looked down. He was silent for several moments. Then he said quietly that if Andy, his dearest friend, his brother almost, wouldn't have him, then why should the people of Platzenhausen want him? Andrew, realizing that Stanwix was hurt, added quickly that the villagers would love him. They would be glad to have him. He really couldn't see why Stanwix was making such a fuss about the whole thing.

Of course he could live in the village.

"But not with you, eh, Andy?"

"Now, Stanwix, I didn't say that. You could live here . . . if you wanted to." Andrew tried not to sound too enthusiastic. The idea of sharing his room with Stanwix wasn't, he thought, a very happy one. Yet he couldn't refuse him outright.

"If I wanted to? Oh, Andy, of course I want to. The thing is I just can't make up my mind about anything." The great bear began to walk back and forth. "It will be so difficult to leave Vivian."

"Difficult?"

"Yes, you see, I have to watch over her. Did you know that witches lose their power when they sleep?"

Andrew looked skeptical.

"Yes, it is true, Andy. I read that in a book." The bear was silent for a while. Then his eyes grew misty and he said, "In the evenings we sit on the porch together—I in my rocking chair, she on the steps—and we talk and watch the moon rise over the forest."

A wave of jealousy swept over Andrew. Suddenly he wished he could trade places with the bear. He would gladly let Stanwix have this room if only he could live in the forest with Vivian.

However, he said, "If it is so difficult to leave her —don't. And stop coming here in the middle of the night and waking me up."

"Andy, don't you see? I have to know. Right now I'm not really sure whether I am a bear or whether I am a man. The bears in the forest won't have me, and I'm not sure whether the people in the village will have me."

"Why shouldn't they have you? There is no reason why they shouldn't." But deep down Andrew wasn't so sure. It seemed very unlikely to him that the people of Platzenhausen would accept a bear as their next-door neighbor.

The bear sat down on the windowsill. "How can you be so sure, Andy? You are just a little boy. How do you know how the villagers will feel toward me?"

Andrew bristled. "I may be only a little boy as you say, but at least I was born one—I didn't have to be made into one."

The bear said nothing. Andrew saw that he had again hurt him and was instantly sorry. He tried to soften his words by saying, "I only meant by that, Stanwix, that I have lived here all my life and I understand these people, and I know that they will come to love you." He wanted to add "as I do," but he couldn't quite say the words.

The bear, meanwhile, was gazing out of the window. "It is growing light," he said worriedly. " I had better go."

"But why?" cried Andrew. "Have you made your decision? Will you stay in the forest?"

"No, no. I must think some more. I must think."

"But, Stanwix—"

"No, no," shouted the great bear. And he leaped out of the window and ran toward the forest.

Andrew watched him go, feeling, it must be admitted, somewhat relieved. He just couldn't understand that bear and he couldn't understand himself. He wished he hadn't said some of those cruel things to Stanwix. He didn't really mean them. Why was he always so cross with him, when he really liked him very much?

He hadn't wanted to lie to Stanwix either. But he hadn't had the heart to tell him that the people of Platzenhausen, who wouldn't even accept their neighbors as friends, would never accept a bear.

Actually he wished this were not so, because if Stanwix were to remain in the village, Andrew could live with Vivian and watch over her when necessary.

Andrew went back to bed. And when he fell asleep again, he had some strange and terrifying dreams which he couldn't remember when he woke up.

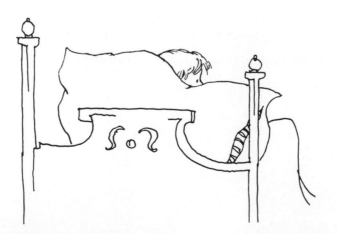

Chapter 11

It was near midnight of the next day, and a large crowd had gathered before the mayor's house. There was a festival atmosphere in the air, and they carried torches and sang patriotic songs. Everyone was filled with excitement at the thought of what was about to happen. In a little while the mayor came out holding a white flag and the bag of orphans' money.

A cheer rang out. "Brave fellow," they cried. "Who else but our mayor would agree to do such a thing for us? Who else but our mayor would be so courageous and so willing to lay down his life for us?" The mayor tried to smile but couldn't quite manage it.

Then the villagers escorted him to the edge of Ebonhausen Forest and wished him well. The mayor walked on, and when he looked back, he saw that he was all alone.

It started to rain. It was dark, so very dark that he could hardly see where he was going. A bolt of lightning showed him the way.

The trees watched him threateningly. In the night they looked like monsters. The rain-soaked branches hung low just over his head, waving at him menacingly when the wind blew.

Fearful bolts of lightning ripped through the sky. And sounds, frightening sounds, filled the air: the roars of the bears, the rustling of the underbrush, the flapping of wings whirring about him. Many times the mayor would have turned back had not a bolt of blue lightning prodded him on. Twice he fell, and his clothes became all muddy and wet.

"This is terrible," said the mayor. The thought of just dropping the money and running for home went through his mind. Yet he could not bring himself to do it. The people of Platzenhausen had put their trust in him. He would not fail them again. He was their mayor. Frightened or not, he had to go on.

It was a long time since he had last walked in these woods. His thoughts flowed back to the days when he was a very young boy, to the days when he had often tramped through the sweet-smelling woods, and to that thrilling day when he first set his eyes on the witch. Yes. Yes. He had been friends with a witch many, many years before. He could remember so clearly those days of excitement and wonders. He could remember all those fearfully wicked things that she had done; the terrors she had caused; the fear and confusion she had spread among the people of Platzenhausen.

And then, like the springing up of a fresh breeze, a new feeling of closeness had swept through the village. The villagers had banded together as one to fight off the evil witch. For once in their lives they had dropped their own petty hatreds and had worked together to help each other.

He remembered that day when the witch, weeping, finally forced to leave, had begged him not to forget her. "For," she had said, "when I return to the place where the witches stay, I can live only as long as somebody, even one person, remembers me. Will you promise? Will you promise always to remember me?" And he had sworn that he would. Then the witch foretold that he would one day become the mayor of Platzenhausen.

The prophecy had come true. Many years later

he was indeed mayor, but by then he had already forgotten his promise. Instead of keeping the witch's image before the people to remind them how they had been drawn together, had fought together and helped each other, he himself had put her out of his mind. Instead of setting a good example for the people to follow, he had soon behaved just as selfishly as the villagers, who had fallen back into their old ways of meanness and spitefulness. He had failed to keep his promise. For it wasn't the secret, as he told Andrew, that he had forgotten. It was the promise he had not kept.

In the distance he saw a light. Slowly the mayor approached it. Soon he could see that it came from the witch's house. Was it his fault that a witch had again come to Platzenhausen? His heart beat violently. Would he be punished for his forgotten promise?

Black smoke erupted from the chimney. An owl hooted frantically. He could see another light go on in the house. And another. And another. She knew that he was coming. The wind tore open the door and it banged back and forth. The mayor nearly fainted with fright. He expected at any moment to be struck down.

But he saw no one. The poor mayor, with his flag and the bag of money, stood before the door not knowing what to do next. The hooting of the owl went on and on.

Gathering what little courage he had left, he raised the bag of money and cried, "Here, here is gold. Take it and leave us in peace."

All was still. The rain stopped. The wind stopped. The mysterious sounds of the forest stopped. And the mayor's legs shook so, he could hardly stand.

He cried out again, "Oh, witch, please leave us alone. I will give you a fortune in money. Please take it. I only demand—"

Then, horror of horrors, the owl swooped out of the house and began to speak, "What? You dare to bring me money? This money which should have gone to the orphanage—you offer it to me? No, no, old man. Your money means nothing to me. You bring me nothing but dead promises. You and your people are selfish and thoughtless. The life of the witch you knew hangs by a thread. She is only a flickering memory. You have forgotten your promise."

A bolt of lightning came from the sky. A terrible, terrible flash. It tore the bag of money from the mayor's hand and hurled its contents into the air.

The mayor ran. He ran and he ran and he ran. The hot coins came tearing through the air after him.

He screamed in fright as he sped through the darkness.

By sheer instinct he found his way back to the village. The villagers who were waiting for his return watched in dismay as the bedraggled figure of their mayor ran howling into his house. In panic they too fled before the searing coins that flew among them. Many of them were burned by the gold pieces. They realized then that they had been wrong to offer the witch the orphans' money. How angry she was. She had flung the money right back at them.

The people of Platzenhausen stayed up most of the night visiting each other and going from house to house to help the wounded. As in the days of the first witch, they found a measure of happiness in helping and comforting one another. They sat together in groups discussing the witch and how to combat her. All sorts of plans were brought forth. But most important, this night the people of Platzenhausen suddenly rediscovered the pleasure that friendship gives. They looked at their neighbors as though for the first time. And they began to like each other.

They returned to their homes. Tomorrow they would gather up the coins and give them to the orphans. And tomorrow there would be more meetings.

The storm began again and it raged for hours. Thunder and lightning and wind tore at the helpless village. Screams filled the air. Surrounded by friends, however, the people were no longer so frightened.

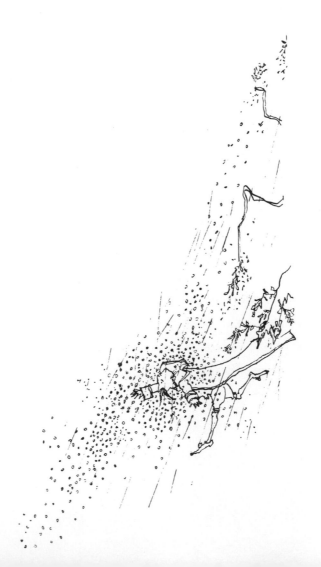

Chapter 12

Andrew was walking alone on the outskirts of the village. It was a week later and he had not seen Vivian all that time. His parents had warned him not to go into the forest again, at least not until the witch was gone. He was on the point of telling them that the witch was his friend and that she would never hurt him. But he didn't. They would not understand.

He could not tell them that deep down in his heart he liked her very much. He, their son, liked a witch. Oh, he knew that she could do terrible things, as she had indeed already done, that she could bring all kinds of terrors to the village. But he knew too that she didn't spit fire, and that she was pretty and could be very sweet, like the time at the fair. And in a way she was doing some good for Platzenhausen.

Before she came the villagers did nothing but eat and sleep and think of no one but themselves. Now, due to Vivian's mischief making, they had become friendlier with each other and were working together more closely than they ever had before.

At that moment Andrew became aware of a little boy walking solemnly beside him. Somehow the boy looked very familiar to him. He had such deep blue eyes and his face was so sad and beautiful. Where had he seen him before? Then Andrew remembered: the boy with the flute.

Andrew grasped him by the arm and cried, "I remember you. You turned us all blue, and then we made you laugh and you disappeared." The little boy nodded sadly. Andrew asked if he were going to turn them all blue again. "No, of course not." The little boy smiled, and it was like the sun peeping over a dark cloud.

Andrew, not really knowing why, felt his heart fill with love for this boy. "What is your name, little boy?" he asked.

And the little boy answered, "Vivian."

A chill ran down Andrew's back. "Vivian?"

"Of course, Andy. Why are you so surprised?"

"But you are a boy."

"Sometimes I like to be a boy."

"But then, when I met you in the forest for the first time, you already knew me."

"Yes, I did, Andy."

"And when the bear, Stanwix, chased us, you could have stopped him by magic at any time."

"Yes, and I did when I saw that you were out of breath."

"Weren't you?"

"Oh, no, I can run all day. I often do."

"Oh, Vivian, you are so wonderful. I love being with you."

The little witch shrugged her shoulders. "Love," she said. "I don't think I know what that word means, Andy. To a witch that word means nothing."

"Will you ever stop being a witch?"

"Never, I suppose. I wouldn't know how to be anything else."

They walked, the two boys, hand in hand.

"I wish I were a witch too," cried Andrew.

Vivian smiled.

"If I were a witch," continued Andrew, "you wouldn't need Stanwix. Then I could watch over you when you are sleeping."

"When I am sleeping?"

"Yes. Stanwix told me that you lose your power when you sleep."

Vivian laughed. "That silly bear, he read that in a book. He believes everything he reads in books, poor thing. No, Andy, it isn't true. But Stanwix believes it so fervently that I haven't the heart to tell him the truth."

"It seems that we all have to lie to Stanwix," said Andrew. "Vivian, why is that bear always so unhappy? After what you did for him, he should be the happiest bear in the world."

"The happiest bear or the happiest man?"

"What do you mean?"

"That's why he isn't happy, Andy. He doesn't know what he is. I knew it would be that way when I gave him that 'wonderful gift,' as he calls it."

"Then why did you do it?" cried Andrew.

"I am a witch, Andy. I have a quick and terrible temper. I was very angry, and that's why I did it. I did not intend to grow so fond of him."

"Change him back into a bear again."

"No, no, I like him the way he is."

The two boys continued walking. Andrew was silent for a long while. Then he said, "Still, I wish I were a witch. I could help you in so many ways."

Vivian smiled. "That's silly," she said. "You must be as you are. You are too kindhearted to be a witch."

"I could be as mean as I wanted to. I could be as mean as—"

"As mean as me?" said Vivian.

"Oh, no, I didn't mean that."

"All right, Andy. We'll see. For the next hour you will have the power of a witch—but only for an hour." Vivian vanished in a puff of smoke.

Andrew stood alone in the street. His whole body tingled. Was he really a witch? Or was this another one of Vivian's practical jokes.

"All right, then," he said. "I'll try. I want to change myself into a big, fierce dog."

Instantly Andrew became a dog.

"It's true. It's true," he cried. "Now I'll show Vivian. I can be as mean as a witch is supposed to be."

Andrew the dog bolted savagely down the street, barking fiercely and scattering the people of Platzenhausen right and left. "Mad dog! Mad dog!" they cried. Andrew snapped and growled viciously at them. How they ran. What fun it was for him to scare everyone so. He almost wished he could always be a dog. Luckily he didn't wish it, because if he had, it would have come true.

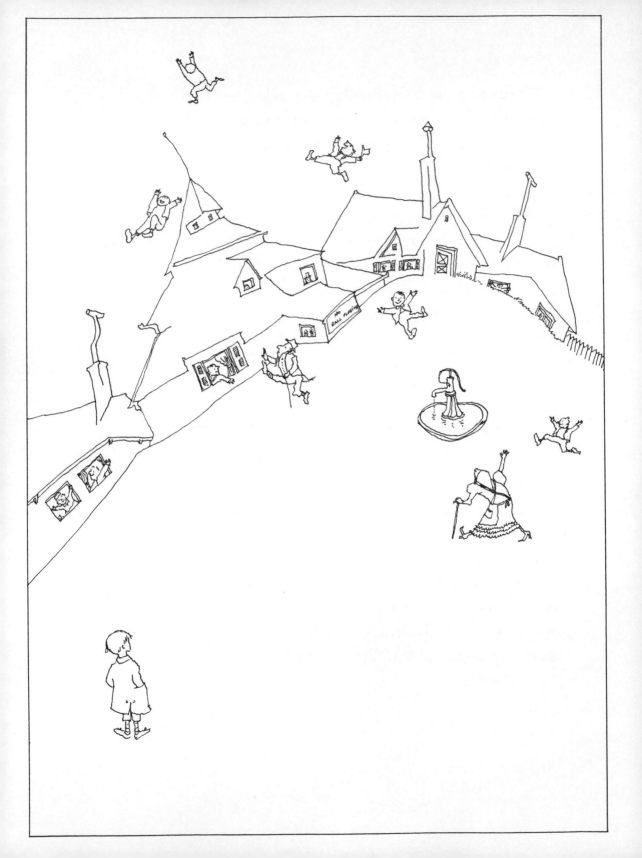

Soon he grew tired of the game and changed back to himself. As he walked down the street several of his friends stopped him and spoke of the terrible dog that had attacked them. Andrew shivered delicately and declared how glad he was that he hadn't seen the dog, because dogs frightened him.

He was really enjoying himself. "Now I think that I'll make everyone as light as a feather."

No sooner said than done. All the people of Platzenhausen began to float in the air. Every step they took bounced them twenty feet high. At first they were terrified, but in a little while they began to like it. It was rather pleasant to float in the air. The children especially enjoyed jumping over buildings.

"That's enough of that," decided Andrew. "Perhaps now, on this hot summer day, we could use some snow. A lot of it."

Down came the snow. In a little while the streets were all covered with it. The villagers scurried to their homes to get their shovels, boots, and sleds.

"How marvelous it is to be a witch," thought Andrew. "I can do anything I want to." As the snowdrifts piled higher and higher Andrew laughed and decided that would be enough. "That's enough snow.

Let it stop now." But it didn't. Down it came, just as before.

"Stop! Stop!" cried Andrew.

It didn't.

Andrew looked at the church clock. His hour was over. He was no longer a witch. He couldn't stop the snowstorm. "Vivian. Vivian," he cried.

There was no answer.

He tried to run through the streets, but he couldn't. The snow came up past his knees. He was stuck in it. What if it never stopped and he and all the villagers were buried in it?

Then he heard the sound of a flute. Twisting himself around, he saw Vivian the boy sitting on a snowdrift.

"Stop the snow," cried Andrew.

Vivian nodded solemnly and the snow stopped falling. The hot sun soon began to melt it.

"Oh, Vivian," wailed Andrew. "What a fool I've been. I've been so cruel to all my friends. I just didn't think. I'm glad I'm not a witch. I'd hate to have to do such terrible things all the time."

Vivian put her flute down and smiled her bewitching smile. "Yes, Andy," she said. "Sometimes it is very

difficult to be a witch." Then she changed herself into
a dazzling white bird and flew away.

Andrew went home feeling very sad.

Chapter 13

It had been decided at another town meeting: The village of Platzenhausen was to be turned into an armed camp. The mad dog and the midsummer snow were the last straw.

Life in the village had become intolerable. The evil witch had turned their lives into a nightmare. They woke up each morning with a numbing, growing fear. Would this be their last day on earth? Would they all be murdered today?

They just could not go on like this anymore. There was only one thing to do. They would have to kill the witch.

With swords, rifles, and sticks they marched up and down the streets searching for her. They patrolled the outskirts of the village. They stood guard on the rooftops, scanning the area with powerful field

glasses. Already plans were being made to storm her house in the woods.

This time they would get rid of the witch for good. They were certain of it. All of the able-bodied men in the village took part, even Mr. Grossenhausen, the man Vivian had changed into a jackass and who was still bewitched. In fact he was the most active of all, galloping here and there and braying whenever he thought he saw the witch. But after three days of vigilance, the villagers could boast only of one wounded rabbit, one man who had shot himself in the toe, and another man who had knocked the head off a scarecrow. But they were not discouraged. They were more than ever determined to carry out their plan.

And their anger at the witch continued to bring them closer together. For just as the ice had melted from them at Lake Merehausen, so did their coldness and meanness melt from them now.

The women set out tables of food. They had cooked their best, their most savory dishes for the heroic soldiers. The men hovered around the tables, tasting the different dishes and loudly declaring their choice for the best cook. The women giggled with pleasure.

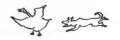

Some children dressed themselves in outlandish costumes and paraded down the street in the bright sunshine to the accompaniment of music and the cheers of the grown-ups.

Andrew was sitting with friends in the village square. The boys who were too young to carry rifles poked fun at those who did. Especially at the mayor, who marched in front of his house with a rifle so heavy that he could barely carry it, let alone fire it. They laughed good-naturedly at his skinny, buckling legs. But Andrew did not laugh.

The boys told stories among themselves about what they would do to the witch, and thought up plans for capturing her. Some of them related how they had actually seen her—how ugly she was, and how wicked and mean. She had flaming eyes, a prodigious nose, and big black wings.

Andrew leaned back and smiled at all this nonsense. He could tell them what she really looked like, but of course they wouldn't believe him. They would rather believe their own silly stories.

He felt a glow of happiness at the thought that Vivian was his friend. He just couldn't imagine why she liked him. But the fact that she did filled him

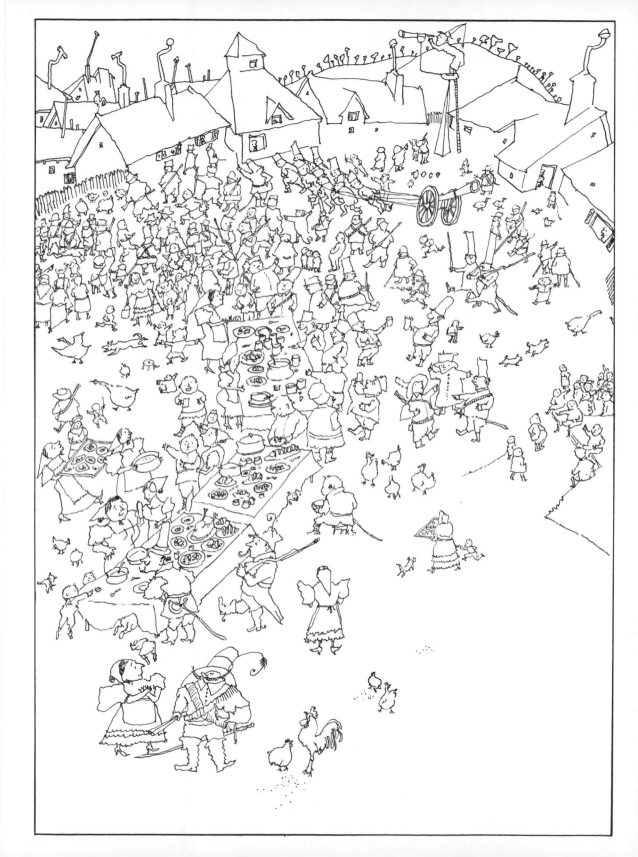

with a sweetness he could hardly describe. The whole world looked beautiful to him; he was certain everyone could see his happiness. He tried hard to listen to what his friends were saying, but his mind kept happily wandering off to that house in the woods.

He watched the men acting like soldiers, more like toy soldiers really. What a waste of time it all was. The little witch was much too powerful for them. How she must be laughing at all their efforts.

Three shots rang out. They came so unexpectedly that everyone stopped in his tracks. Andrew shivered. A dark shadow sped across the sky, and it began to rain in large drops.

For several moments everything was still. Then the sound of cheering could be heard in the distance. Andrew tried to see over the heads of the gathering villagers, but he was too small.

The cheering grew louder and louder and louder. Soon a group of men waving their rifles, led by Mr. Grossenhausen, came up to the mayor. The men were all shouting, and at first they could not be understood. As they came closer Andrew heard them cry, "We've killed the witch."

The villagers burst into a mighty "Hurrah!" and

84

the mayor hugged the men, including Mr. Grossenhausen. But were they sure? Were they absolutely
certain it was the witch they had killed? Andrew
strained to listen.

Certainly they were sure. They had seen the
witch with their own eyes, and they had shot her.
There was no doubt.

Andrew leaned against a tree for support. It
couldn't be true. He knew it. But still his heart
pounded furiously. The rain grew heavier. The air felt
oppressive. The mayor caught Andrew's eye and smiled
a little sadly.

"Tell us about it," cried the villagers.

Mr. Grossenhausen began to bray, but no one
could understand him. One of the men with him leaned
on his rifle and said, "We were patrolling near the
forest when we heard a great thrashing about in the
underbrush. I'll admit we were very frightened, but
we held our ground. And then . . . then—"

"And then—?" prodded the rapt villagers.

"And then from the forest came this huge
monster."

"Oh," they all cried.

"This monster—hairy and terrible, with fierce

teeth and glassy eyes—tried to conceal itself behind a tree."

"Horrors," they wailed.

"Mr. Grossenhausen began to bray very loudly, and we knew at once it was the witch. For who should know her better than Mr. Grossenhausen, who is under her spell?"

"True, true," they agreed.

"So we pointed our rifles at it—the witch—and then . . . and then . . . it spoke to us."

"Oh, no. Oh, no."

"It spoke to us." The man wiped his brow.

"Go on. Go on."

"It said, 'No, no. Don't raise your rifles at me. I am a man like you.' But we shouted back, 'No, you are the witch.' "

"Bravo!"

"But this thing, this horror, laughed. Then it said, 'Witch? There is no witch, only an angel.' "

"The deceitful thing," they muttered.

"And then this monster—the witch—raised both its terrible arms and approached us, saying, 'See, I am one of you. Let us embrace each other. Let us—' "

"Horrors," they protested.

"We raised our rifles and fired three times. The

terrible thing fell before us with a hideous roar. Then it was still."

"Bravo! Bravo!" They applauded.

A great roll of thunder could be heard. The rain fell furiously. But the villagers didn't mind. They formed a ring around their heroes and danced and sang.

Andrew, turning away so that no one would see him, leaned against a tree and burst into tears. Stanwix, poor Stanwix, was dead.

Just then the good people of Platzenhausen raised a new shout of joy. Mr. Grossenhausen's long ears had vanished. His tail had disappeared. He was a man once more.

Indeed . . . indeed . . . the witch must be dead.

Chapter 14

Not until the following day could Andrew go to the forest. The wind tore at his raincoat as he hurried to the witch's house. The long storm had turned the woods into a sea of mud, and it was treacherous going. It was as though invisible fingers clutched at his shoes as they sank, sometimes ankle deep, into the mud. But he hardly noticed. His heart was filled with too many things. Sadness for poor Stanwix. Happiness and relief that it wasn't Vivian who had been shot.

Of course he wouldn't take part in the celebration that was still going on in Platzenhausen. There they were having a great feast in honor of the men who had killed what they thought was the witch. Even at this distance he could hear the village brass and wood-wind orchestra playing at the festivities. It always did play loudly. But not, he remembered, loudly enough to drown out the somber sound of the flute when they were trying to cheer up the little blue boy. That all seemed so long ago. That strange day, the beginning of his wonderful adventure. And now, was it all over? He knew how the other witch had been driven away. Would it be the same with Vivian? No! He refused to believe it. Stanwix was, after all, only a bear. There would be many happy, exciting days ahead.

As for the villagers, wouldn't they be surprised? He wondered what they would do when they learned that the witch was still very much alive and ready, he hoped, to start playing her tricks again. He wondered what terribly outrageous ideas she was thinking up right now. Oh, yes, they would have lots of fun together.

Then Andrew thought about the surprise visit the mayor had made to his house the night before. How gently the old man had spoken to him. Over tea, the mayor had invited Andrew to come to his office whenever the boy felt like it, to read the mayor's books and papers, to look at his ship model collection. In fact, Andrew was to make himself at home there. Andrew's parents had been overwhelmed with pleasure, and he himself had been struck by the goodness of the mayor. He had wondered if the old man really knew about him and the little witch. But Mayor Shrekenhausen had kept wonderfully silent, and Andrew never found out for sure.

At last he arrived at the house in the woods. The rocking chair stood empty on the porch, the wind pushing it to and fro. Andrew shuddered as he went inside.

He walked through the lonely house, room by room. There was no one. He called, "Vivian. Vivian."

There was no answer.

He climbed the stairs. "Vivian. Vivian."

Silence.

He went up to the attic. It was dark and cold and forbidding there. In the corner on the floor sat the little witch with tears, a shower of them, rolling down her pale cheeks. She looked so small and so forlorn. Andrew knelt before her. "Oh, Vivian, don't cry."

She looked at him with brimming eyes. "Crying? Am I crying?"

Andrew could hardly keep his own tears back. "Yes, dear Vivian," he said, taking her hand.

"I—I never cried before."

"Yes, but Stanwix is dead. That is why you are crying."

"Yes, yes, I suppose so." Vivian looked away, at

the rain pounding against the window. Then she said, "But there is something else too."

"Something else?"

"Here, feel my nose."

It was warm like his own.

"You see," she said. "I am losing my power. I should have left yesterday."

"Yesterday?"

There was silence for a moment, then the little witch said, "You know, Andy, you must know that whenever a witch causes the death of an innocent soul, she loses all her power and must return to where she came from."

"Yes, but Stanwix was a bear."

"I turned him into a man."

"But you are a witch. You can do anything. We can have so much fun together."

Vivian shook her head. "No, no, Andy. I have committed a dreadful sin, and I must return and await my fate. I've been waiting here all night for you, Andy. I didn't want to leave without seeing you again. I wanted to tell you that I never, never meant Stanwix to get hurt. At first, as you know, I created him out of spitefulness, but soon I got to like him just as I like you. I thought I would be able to protect him. I never meant this to happen."

"Oh, I know that you would never want to hurt Stanwix. I know that. But please, Vivian, don't go. I will miss you so much." He clasped her hand tightly. The thought of life without the little witch was almost too much to endure.

No longer would the air around him be filled with enchantment. No longer would he be someone special with a beautiful secret. He would be lonely, lonely, lonely. Even with his friends, even with his parents whom he loved, his life now would be sad and still. The magic would be gone.

"Please don't go," he pleaded.

"I have to, Andy. I really have no choice. But you must promise never to forget me."

"Forget you? How could I ever forget you."

"You must never, Andy. I can live only so long as someone remembers me."

"I'll never forget you, Vivian. And I'll see to it that everyone in the village remembers you too. Forever."

Her eyes filled with tears again.

"The people here have changed since you've

come," said Andrew. "They've learned to like each other and to help each other."

"Someday you will have the power to help them, Andy."

"Will I be a witch then?"

Vivian smiled. "No, Andy," she said. "The trust the people will have in you will give you the power. You will grow up to be a great man. You will be the mayor of Platzenhausen. That is why I picked you, out of all the people of Platzenhausen, to be my friend."

"Picked me?"

"Yes. I made you come and look for me when I was the blue boy."

And then, as Andrew watched helplessly, she slowly, slowly disappeared.

Many, many years went by, and the prophecy of the witch came true. Andrew, now old, gray, and with a fine moustache, was indeed the mayor of Platzenhausen.

Mayor Andrew Papenhausen, as you have no doubt read in your history books, was one of the best mayors the village ever had. He ruled with understanding and kindness. And if, sometimes, he happened to find one of the old villagers falling back into spiteful ways, he made sure to remind him of the day the witch came and turned the village blue. He also saw to it that the story of the little witch was told and retold, by those who remembered it, to children and grandchildren down the generations just as I am telling it to you now, so that Vivian would not be forgotten.

Often, even in the wintertime when the trees were bare and the sky was gray, he would walk in the forest, remembering the exciting days with Vivian and Stanwix. As he passed her house he would look at the chimney, half hoping to see wisps of smoke rising from it.

But he never, never did.

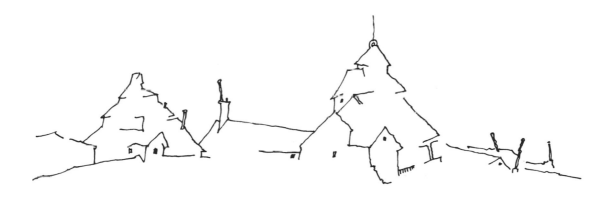